Henry Wadsworth Longfellow

The hanging of the crane and other poems of the home

Henry Wadsworth Longfellow

The hanging of the crane and other poems of the home

ISBN/EAN: 9783337118310

Printed in Europe, USA, Canada, Australia, Japan

Cover: Foto ©Andreas Hilbeck / pixelio.de

More available books at **www.hansebooks.com**

THE HANGING OF THE CRANE

AND OTHER POEMS OF THE HOME
BY HENRY WADSWORTH LONGFELLOW

ILLUSTRATED

BOSTON AND NEW YORK
HOUGHTON, MIFFLIN AND COMPANY
The Riverside Press, Cambridge
M DCCC XCIV

The Riverside Press, Cambridge, Mass., U. S. A.
Electrotyped and Printed by H. O. Houghton & Co.

Contents

List of Illustrations

The Hanging of the Crane

HE lights are out, and gone are
all the guests
That thronging came with mer-
riment and jests
To celebrate the Hanging of the Crane
In the new house, — into the night are
gone ;
But still the fire upon the hearth burns on,
And I alone remain.

O fortunate, O happy day,
When a new household finds its place
Among the myriad homes of earth,

Like a new star just sprung to birth,
And rolled on its harmonious way
Into the boundless realms of space !

So said the guests in speech and song,
As in the chimney, burning bright,
We hung the iron crane to-night,
And merry was the feast and long.

II

AND now I sit and muse on what may
be,
And in my vision see, or seem to see,
  Through floating vapors interfused with
    light,
Shapes indeterminate, that gleam and
    fade,
As shadows passing into deeper shade
    Sink and elude the sight.

.

For two alone, there in the hall,
Is spread the table round and small ;
Upon the polished silver shine
The evening lamps, but, more divine,
The light of love shines over all ;
Of love, that says not mine and thine,
But ours, for ours is thine and mine.

They want no guests, to come between
Their tender glances like a screen,
And tell them tales of land and sea,
And whatsoever may betide
The great, forgotten world outside ;
They want no guests ; they needs must be
Each other's own best company.

III

THE picture fades ; as at a village fair
    A showman's views, dissolving into
       air,
Again appear transfigured on the screen,
So in my fancy this ; and now once more,
In part transfigured, through the open
       door
    Appears the selfsame scene.

Seated, I see the two again,
But not alone ; they entertain
A little angel unaware,
With face as round as is the moon ;
A royal guest with flaxen hair,
Who, throned upon his lofty chair,
Drums on the table with his spoon,
Then drops it careless on the floor,
To grasp at things unseen before.

Are these celestial manners ? these
The ways that win, the arts that please ?
Ah yes ; consider well the guest,
And whatsoe'er he does seems best ;
He ruleth by the right divine
Of helplessness, so lately born
In purple chambers of the morn,
As sovereign over thee and thine.
He speaketh not ; and yet there lies
A conversation in his eyes ;
The golden silence of the Greek,
The gravest wisdom of the wise,
Not spoken in language, but in looks
More legible than printed books,
As if he could but would not speak.
And now, O monarch absolute,
Thy power is put to proof ; for, lo !
Resistless, fathomless, and slow,
The nurse comes rustling like the sea,
And pushes back thy chair and thee,
And so good night to King Canute.

IV

A S one who walking in a forest sees
A lovely landscape through the
parted trees,
Then sees it not, for boughs that inter-
vene ;
Or as we see the moon sometimes revealed
Through drifting clouds, and then again
concealed,
So I behold the scene.

There are two guests at table now ;
The king, deposed and older grown,
No longer occupies the throne, —
The crown is on his sister's brow ;
A Princess from the Fairy Isles,
The very pattern girl of girls,
All covered and embowered in curls,
Rose-tinted from the Isle of Flowers,

6

And sailing with soft, silken sails
From far-off Dreamland into ours.
Above their bowls with rims of blue
Four azure eyes of deeper hue
Are looking, dreamy with delight;
Limpid as planets that emerge
Above the ocean's rounded verge,
Soft-shining through the summer night.
Steadfast they gaze, yet nothing see
Beyond the horizon of their bowls;
Nor care they for the world that rolls
With all its freight of troubled souls
Into the days that are to be.

V

AGAIN the tossing boughs shut out
the scene,
Again the drifting vapors intervene,

And the moon's pallid disk is hidden
    quite ;
And now I see the table wider grown,
As round a pebble into water thrown
    Dilates a ring of light.

I see the table wider grown,
I see it garlanded with guests,
As if fair Ariadne's Crown
Out of the sky had fallen down ;
Maidens within whose tender breasts
A thousand restless hopes and fears,
Forth reaching to the coming years,
Flutter awhile, then quiet lie,
Like timid birds that fain would fly,
But do not dare to leave their nests ; —
And youths, who in their strength elate
Challenge the van and front of fate,
Eager as champions to be
In the divine knight-errantry
Of youth, that travels sea and land

Seeking adventures, or pursues,
Through cities, and through solitudes
Frequented by the lyric Muse,
The phantom with the beckoning hand,
That still allures and still eludes.
O sweet illusions of the brain !
O sudden thrills of fire and frost !
The world is bright while ye remain,
And dark and dead when ye are lost !

VI

THE meadow-brook, that seemeth to
    stand still,
Quickens its current as it nears the mill ;
    And so the stream of Time that lingereth
In level places, and so dull appears,
Runs with a swifter current as it nears
    The gloomy mills of Death.

And now, like the magician's scroll,
That in the owner's keeping shrinks
With every wish he speaks or thinks,
Till the last wish consumes the whole,
The table dwindles, and again
I see the two alone remain.
The crown of stars is broken in parts ;
Its jewels, brighter than the day,
Have one by one been stolen away
To shine in other homes and hearts.
One is a wanderer now afar
In Ceylon or in Zanzibar,
Or sunny regions of Cathay ;
And one is in the boisterous camp
Mid clink of arms and horses' tramp,
And battle's terrible array.
I see the patient mother read,
With aching heart, of wrecks that float
Disabled on those seas remote,
Or of some great heroic deed
On battle-fields, where thousands bleed

To lift one hero into fame.
Anxious she bends her graceful head
Above these chronicles of pain,
And trembles with a secret dread
Lest there among the drowned or slain
She find the one beloved name.

VII

AFTER a day of cloud and wind and
rain
Sometimes the setting sun breaks out
again,
And, touching all the darksome woods
with light,
Smiles on the fields, until they laugh and
sing,
Then like a ruby from the horizon's ring
Drops down into the night.

What see I now?   The night is fair,
The storm of grief, the clouds of care,
The wind, the rain, have passed away ;
The lamps are lit, the fires burn bright,
The house is full of life and light :
It is the Golden Wedding day.
The guests come thronging in once more,
Quick footsteps sound along the floor,
The trooping children crowd the stair,
And in and out and everywhere
Flashes along the corridor
The sunshine of their golden hair.
On the round table in the hall
Another Ariadne's Crown
Out of the sky hath fallen down ;
More than one Monarch of the Moon
Is drumming with his silver spoon ;
The light of love shines over all.

O fortunate, O happy day !
The people sing, the people say.

The ancient bridegroom and the bride,
Smiling contented and serene
Upon the blithe, bewildering scene,
Behold, well pleased, on every side
Their forms and features multiplied,
As the reflection of a light
Between two burnished mirrors gleams,
Or lamps upon a bridge at night
Stretch on and on before the sight,
Till the long vista endless seems.

The Children's Hour

ETWEEN the dark and the day-
   light,
   When the night is beginning to
   lower,
Comes a pause in the day's occupations,
   That is known as the Children's Hour.

I hear in the chamber above me
   The patter of little feet,
The sound of a door that is opened,
   And voices soft and sweet.

From my study I see in the lamplight,
   Descending the broad hall stair,
Grave Alice, and laughing Allegra,
   And Edith with golden hair.

A whisper, and then a silence:
  Yet I know by their merry eyes
They are plotting and planning together
  To take me by surprise.

A sudden rush from the stairway,
  A sudden raid from the hall!
By three doors left unguarded
  They enter my castle wall!

They climb up into my turret
  O'er the arms and back of my chair;
If I try to escape, they surround me;
  They seem to be everywhere.

They almost devour me with kisses,
  Their arms about me entwine,
Till I think of the Bishop of Bingen
  In his Mouse-Tower on the Rhine!

Do you think, O blue-eyed banditti,
  Because you have scaled the wall,
Such an old mustache as I am
  Is not a match for you all !

I have you fast in my fortress,
  And will not let you depart,
But put you down into the dungeon
  In the round-tower of my heart.

And there will I keep you forever,
  Yes, forever and a day,
Till the walls shall crumble to ruin,
  And moulder in dust away !

To a Child

DEAR child! how radiant on thy
    mother's knee,
  With merry-making eyes and
    jocund smiles,
Thou gazest at the painted tiles,
Whose figures grace,
With many a grotesque form and face,
The ancient chimney of thy nursery!
The lady with the gay macaw,
The dancing girl, the grave bashaw
With bearded lip and chin ;
And, leaning idly o'er his gate,
Beneath the imperial fan of state,
The Chinese mandarin.

With what a look of proud command
Thou shakest in thy little hand

The coral rattle with its silver bells,
Making a merry tune !
Thousands of years in Indian seas
That coral grew, by slow degrees,
Until some deadly and wild monsoon
Dashed it on Coromandel's sand !
Those silver bells
Reposed of yore,
As shapeless ore,
Far down in the deep-sunken wells
Of darksome mines,
In some obscure and sunless place,
Beneath huge Chimborazo's base,
Or Potosí's o'erhanging pines !
And thus for thee, O little child,
Through many a danger and escape,
The tall ships passed the stormy cape ;
For thee in foreign lands remote,
Beneath a burning, tropic clime,
The Indian peasant, chasing the wild
    goat,

Himself as swift and wild,
In falling, clutched the frail arbute,
The fibres of whose shallow root,
Uplifted from the soil, betrayed
The silver veins beneath it laid,
The buried treasures of the miser, Time.

But, lo ! thy door is left ajar !
Thou hearest footsteps from afar !
And, at the sound,
Thou turnest round
With quick and questioning eyes,
Like one, who, in a foreign land,
Beholds on every hand
Some source of wonder and surprise !
And, restlessly, impatiently,
Thou strivest, strugglest, to be free.

The four walls of thy nursery
Are now like prison walls to thee.
No more thy mother's smiles,

No more the painted tiles,
Delight thee, nor the playthings on the
floor,
That won thy little, beating heart be-
fore ;
Thou strugglest for the open door.

Through these once solitary halls
Thy pattering footstep falls.
The sound of thy merry voice
Makes the old walls
Jubilant, and they rejoice
With the joy of thy young heart,
O'er the light of whose gladness
No shadows of sadness
From the sombre background of memory
start.

Once, ah, once, within these walls,
One whom memory oft recalls,
The Father of his Country, dwelt.

And yonder meadows broad and damp
The fires of the besieging camp
Encircled with a burning belt.
Up and down these echoing stairs,
Heavy with the weight of cares,
Sounded his majestic tread ;
Yes, within this very room
Sat he in those hours of gloom,
Weary both in heart and head.

But what are these grave thoughts to
      thee ?
Out, out ! into the open air !
Thy only dream is liberty,
Thou carest little how or where.
I see thee eager at thy play,
Now shouting to the apples on the tree,
With cheeks as round and red as they ;
And now among the yellow stalks,
Among the flowering shrubs and plants,
As restless as the bee.

'

Along the garden walks,
The tracks of thy small carriage-wheels
    I trace ;
And see at every turn how they efface
Whole villages of sand-roofed tents,
That rise like golden domes
Above the cavernous and secret homes
Of wandering and nomadic tribes of ants.
Ah, cruel little Tamerlane,
Who, with thy dreadful reign,
Dost persecute and overwhelm
These hapless Troglodytes of thy realm !

What ! tired already ! with those suppli-
    ant looks,
And voice more beautiful than a poet's
    books,
Or murmuring sound of water as it flows,
Thou comest back to parley with repose !
This rustic seat in the old apple-tree,
With its o'erhanging golden canopy

Of leaves illuminate with autumnal hues,
And shining with the argent light of
    dews,
Shall for a season be our place of rest.
Beneath us, like an oriole's pendent nest,
From which the laughing birds have taken
    wing,
By thee abandoned, hangs thy vacant
    swing.
Dream-like the waters of the river gleam ;
A sailless vessel drops adown the stream,
And like it, to a sea as wide and deep,
Thou driftest gently down the tides of
    sleep.

O child ! O new-born denizen
Of life's great city ! on thy head
The glory of the morn is shed,
Like a celestial benison !
Here at the portal thou dost stand,
And with thy little hand

Of leaves illuminate with autumnal hues,
And shining with the argent light of
dews,
Shall for a season be our place of rest.
Beneath us, like an oriole's pendent nest,
From which the laughing birds have taken
wing,
By thee abandoned, hangs thy vacant
swing.
Dream-like the waters of the river gleam ;
A sailless vessel drops adown the stream,
And like it, to a sea as wide and deep,
Thou driftest gently down the tides of
sleep.

O child ! O new-born denizen
Of life's great city ! on thy head
The glory of the morn is shed,
Like a celestial benison !
Here at the portal thou dost stand,
And with thy little hand

Thou openest the mysterious gate
Into the future's undiscovered land.
I see its valves expand,
As at the touch of Fate !
Into those realms of love and hate,
Into that darkness blank and drear,
By some prophetic feeling taught,
I launch the bold, adventurous thought,
Freighted with hope and fear ;
As upon subterranean streams,
In caverns unexplored and dark,
Men sometimes launch a fragile bark,
Laden with flickering fire,
And watch its swift-receding beams,
Until at length they disappear,
And in the distant dark expire.

By what astrology of fear or hope
Dare I to cast thy horoscope !
Like the new moon thy life appears ;
A little strip of silver light,

And widening outward into night
The shadowy disk of future years;
And yet upon its outer rim,
A luminous circle, faint and dim,
And scarcely visible to us here,
Rounds and completes the perfect
      sphere;
A prophecy and intimation,
A pale and feeble adumbration,
Of the great world of light, that lies
Behind all human destinies.

Ah! if thy fate, with anguish fraught,
Should be to wet the dusty soil
With the hot tears and sweat of toil, —
To struggle with imperious thought,
Until the overburdened brain,
Weary with labor, faint with pain,
Like a jarred pendulum, retain
Only its motion, not its power, —
Remember, in that perilous hour,

When most afflicted and oppressed,
From labor there shall come forth rest.

And if a more auspicious fate
On thy advancing steps await,
Still let it ever be thy pride
To linger by the laborer's side ;
With words of sympathy or song
To cheer the dreary march along
Of the great army of the poor,
O'er desert sand, o'er dangerous moor.
Nor to thyself the task shall be
Without reward ; for thou shalt learn
The wisdom early to discern
True beauty in utility ;
As great Pythagoras of yore,
Standing beside the blacksmith's door,
And hearing the hammers, as they smote
The anvils with a different note,
Stole from the varying tones, that hung
Vibrant on every iron tongue,

The secret of the sounding wire,
And formed the seven-chorded lyre.

Enough ! I will not play the Seer ;
I will no longer strive to ope
The mystic volume, where appear
The herald Hope, forerunning Fear,
And Fear, the pursuivant of Hope.
Thy destiny remains untold ;
For, like Acestes' shaft of old,
The swift thought kindles as it flies,
And burns to ashes in the skies.

Maidenhood

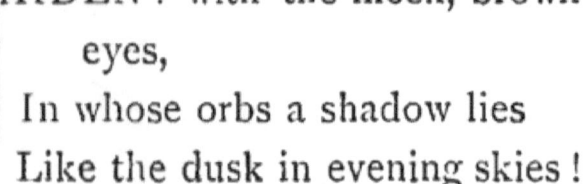AIDEN ! with the meek, brown
eyes,
In whose orbs a shadow lies
Like the dusk in evening skies !

Thou whose locks outshine the sun,
Golden tresses, wreathed in one,
As the braided streamlets run !

Standing, with reluctant feet,
Where the brook and river meet,
Womanhood and childhood fleet !

Gazing, with a timid glance,
On the brooklet's swift advance,
On the river's broad expanse !

Deep and still, that gliding stream
Beautiful to thee must seem,
As the river of a dream.

Then why pause with indecision,
When bright angels in thy vision
Beckon thee to fields Elysian?

Seest thou shadows sailing by,
As the dove, with startled eye,
Sees the falcon's shadow fly?

Hearest thou voices on the shore,
That our ears perceive no more,
Deafened by the cataract's roar?

Oh, thou child of many prayers!
Life   hath   quicksands, — Life   hath
.   snares!
Care and age come unawares!

Like the swell of some sweet tune,
Morning rises into noon,
May glides onward into June.

Childhood is the bough, where slumbered
Birds and blossoms many-numbered ; —
Age, that bough with snows encum-
bered.

Gather, then, each flower that grows,
When the young heart overflows,
To embalm that tent of snows.

Bear a lily in thy hand ;
Gates of brass cannot withstand
One touch of that magic wand.

Bear through sorrow, wrong, and ruth,
In thy heart the dew of youth,
On thy lips the smile of truth.

Oh, that dew, like balm, shall steal
Into wounds that cannot heal,
Even as sleep our eyes doth seal;

And that smile, like sunshine, dart
Into many a sunless heart,
For a smile of God thou art.

The Castle-Builder

 GENTLE boy, with soft and
silken locks,
A dreamy boy, with brown and
tender eyes,
A castle-builder, with his wooden blocks,
And towers that touch imaginary skies.

A fearless rider on his father's knee,
An eager listener unto stories told
At the Round Table of the nursery,
Of heroes and adventures manifold.

There will be other towers for thee to build ;
There will be other steeds for thee to
ride ;
There will be other legends, and all filled
With greater marvels and more glorified.

Build on, and make thy castles high and
    fair,
  Rising and reaching upward to the
    skies ;
Listen to voices in the upper air,
  Nor lose thy simple faith in mysteries.

Weariness

LITTLE feet ! that such long
  years
Must wander on through hopes
  and fears,
  Must ache and bleed beneath your load ;
I, nearer to the wayside inn
Where toil shall cease and rest begin,
  Am weary, thinking of your road !

O little hands ! that, weak or strong,
Have still to serve or rule so long,
  Have still so long to give or ask ;
I, who so much with book and pen
Have toiled among my fellow-men,
  Am weary, thinking of your task.

O little hearts ! that throb and beat
With such impatient, feverish heat,
  Such limitless and strong desires ;
Mine, that so long has glowed and burned,
With passions into ashes turned
  Now covers and conceals its fires.

O little souls ! as pure and white
And crystalline as rays of light
  Direct from heaven, their source divine ;
Refracted through the mist of years,
How red my setting sun appears,
  How lurid looks this soul of mine !

EAFLESS are the trees; their
      purple branches
    Spread themselves abroad, like
      reefs of coral,
  Rising silent
In the Red Sea of the winter sunset.

From the hundred chimneys of the village,
Like the Afreet in the Arabian story,
    Smoky columns
Tower aloft into the air of amber.

At the window winks the flickering fire-
    light;
Here and there the lamps of evening glim-
    mer,

Social watch-fires
Answering one another through the darkness.

On the hearth the lighted logs are glow-
ing,
And like Ariel in the cloven pine-tree
For its freedom
Groans and sighs the air imprisoned in
them.

By the fireside there are old men seated,
Seeing ruined cities in the ashes,
Asking sadly
Of the Past what it can ne'er restore them.

By the fireside there are youthful dream-
ers,
Building castles fair, with stately stairways,
Asking blindly
Of the Future what it cannot give them.

In his farthest wanderings still he sees it;
Hears the talking flame, the answering
    night-wind,
      As he heard them
When he sat with those who were, but are
    not.

Happy he whom neither wealth nor fash-
    ion,
Nor the march of the encroaching city,
      Drives an exile
From the hearth of his ancestral home-
    stead.

We may build more splendid habitations,
Fill our rooms with paintings and with
    sculptures,
      But we cannot
Buy with gold the old associations!

Children

COME to me, O ye children!
　　For I hear you at your play,
　And the questions that per-
　　plexed me
Have vanished quite away.

Ye open the eastern windows,
　That look towards the sun,
Where thoughts are singing swallows
　And the brooks of morning run.

In your hearts are the birds and the sun-
　　shine,
　In your thoughts the brooklet's flow,
But in mine is the wind of Autumn
　And the first fall of the snow.

Ah ! what would the world be to us
  If the children were no more?
We should dread the desert behind us
  Worse than the dark before.

What the leaves are to the forest,
  With light and air for food,
Ere their sweet and tender juices
  Have been hardened into wood, —

That to the world are children ;
  Through them it feels the glow
Of a brighter and sunnier climate
  Than reaches the trunks below.

Come to me, O ye children !
  And whisper in my ear
What the birds and the winds are sing-
    ing
  In your sunny atmosphere.

For what are all our contrivings,
  And the wisdom of our books,
When compared with your caresses,
  And the gladness of your looks?

Ye are better than all the ballads
  That ever were sung or said;
For ye are living poems,
  And all the rest are dead.

Resignation

THERE is no flock, however watched and tended,
But one dead lamb is there !
There is no fireside, howsoe'er defended,
But has one vacant chair !

The air is full of farewells to the dying,
And mournings for the dead ;
The heart of Rachel, for her children crying,
Will not be comforted !

Let us be patient ! These severe afflictions
Not from the ground arise,

But oftentimes celestial benedictions
   Assume this dark disguise.

We see but dimly through the mists and
      vapors ;
   Amid these earthly damps
What seem to us but sad, funereal tapers
   May be heaven's distant lamps.

There is no Death ! What seems so is
      transition ;
   This life of mortal breath
Is but a suburb of the life elysian,
   Whose portal we call Death.

She is not dead, — the child of our affec-
      tion, —
   But gone unto that school
Where she no longer needs our poor pro-
      tection,
   And Christ himself doth rule.

In that great cloister's stillness and se-
    clusion,
  By guardian angels led,
Safe from temptation, safe from sin's pol-
    lution,
  She lives, whom we call dead.

Day after day we think what she is doing
  In those bright realms of air ;
Year after year, her tender steps pursuing,
  Behold her grown more fair.

Thus do we walk with her, and keep un-
    broken
  The bond which nature gives,
Thinking that our remembrance, though
    unspoken,
  May reach her where she lives.

Not as a child shall we again behold her ;
  For when with raptures wild

In our embraces we again enfold her,
  She will not be a child ;

But a fair maiden, in her Father's mansion,
  Clothed with celestial grace ;
And beautiful with all the soul's expansion
  Shall we behold her face.

And though at times impetuous with emo-
      tion
  And anguish long suppressed,
The swelling heart heaves moaning like
      the ocean,
  That cannot be at rest, —

We will be patient, and assuage the feel-
      ing
  We may not wholly stay ;
By silence sanctifying, not concealing,
  The grief that must have way.

Then stay at home, my heart, and rest;
The bird is safest in its nest;
O'er all that flutter their wings and fly
A hawk is hovering in the sky;
    To stay at home is best.

Notes

THE HANGING OF THE CRANE. "One
morning in the spring of 1867," writes Mr. T.
B. Aldrich, "Mr. Longfellow came to the little home in Pinckney Street, [Boston,] where
we had set up housekeeping in the light of
our honeymoon. As we lingered a moment
at the dining-room door, Mr. Longfellow turn-
ing to me said, 'Ah, Mr. Aldrich, your small
round table will not always be closed. By
and by you will find new young faces cluster-
ing about it; as years go on, leaf after leaf
will be added until the time comes when the
young guests will take flight, one by one, to
build nests of their own elsewhere. Grad-
ually the long table will shrink to a circle
again, leaving two old people sitting there
alone together. This is the story of life, the
sweet and pathetic poem of the fireside.

Make an idyl of it. I give the idea to you.' Several months afterward, I received a note from Mr. Longfellow in which he expressed a desire to use this *motif* in case I had done nothing in the matter. The theme was one peculiarly adapted to his sympathetic handling, and out of it grew *The Hanging of the Crane*." Just when the poem was written does not appear, but its first publication was in the *New York Ledger*, March 28, 1874. Mr. Longfellow's old friend, Mr. Sam. Ward, had heard the poem, and offered to secure it for Mr. Robert Bonner, the proprietor of the *Ledger*, "touched," as he wrote to Mr. Longfellow, "by your kindness to poor ——, and haunted by the idea of increasing handsomely your noble charity fund." Mr. Bonner paid the poet the sum of three thousand dollars for this poem.

To a Child. This poem was begun October 2, 1845, and on the 13th of the next month Mr. Longfellow noted in his diary:

" Walked in the garden and tried to finish the *Ode to a Child;* but could not find the exact expressions I wanted, to round and complete the whole." After the publication of the volume containing it, he wrote : " The poem *To a Child* and *The Old Clock on the Stairs* seem to be the favorites. This is the best answer to my assailants." Possibly the charge was made then as frequently afterward that his poetry was an echo of foreign scenes. It is at any rate noticeable that in this poem he first strongly expressed that domestic sentiment which was to be so conspicuous in his after work. It will be remembered that he was married to Miss Appleton in July, 1843, and his second child was born at the time when he was writing this ode. Five years later he made the following entry in his diary : " Some years ago, writing an *Ode to a Child,* I spoke of

The buried treasures of the miser, Time.

What was my astonishment to-day, in reading

for the first time in my life Wordsworth's beautiful ode *On the Power of Sound*, to read

All treasures hoarded by the miser, 'Time."

MAIDENHOOD. When writing to his father of the appearance of his new volume of poems, Mr. Longfellow said : " I think the last two pieces the best, — perhaps as good as anything I have written." These pieces were *Maidenhood* and *Excelsior*. The former was published in the *Southern Literary Messenger* for January, 1842.

THE GOLDEN MILE-STONE. " December 20, 1854. The weather is ever so cold. The landscape looks dreary ; but the sunset and twilight are resplendent. Sketch out a poem, *The Golden Mile-Stone*."

CHILDREN. " February 1, 1849. I wrote another poem to-day, — on the children whom I heard rejoicing overhead while I sat below here in rather melancholy mood."

RESIGNATION. Written in the autumn of
1848, after the death of his little daughter
Fanny. There is a passage in the poet's
diary, under date of November 12th, in which
he says: " I feel very sad to-day. I miss very
much my dear little Fanny. An inappeasa-
ble longing to see her comes over me at times,
which I can hardly control."